"Richard Barre touches the soul. He is simply one of the best."

—HARLAN COBEN

best-selling author of *Gone For Good* and *Tell No One*

"The sheer beauty and strength of Barre's writing gives a glow of redemption that is extremely rare in any kind of fiction."

—*CHICAGO TRIBUNE*

"Barre's writing is lean and thoughtful and muscular."

—ROBERT CRAIS

best-selling author of *Hostage* and *L.A. Requiem*

"Although known as a writer of outstanding detective novels, Richard Barre has written a suspense story of extraordinary poignancy that will keep readers at the edge of their seats as they dry their eyes."

—OTTO PENZLER

The Mysterious Bookshop

The Star

The Star

✧

Richard Barre

Foreword by Michael Connelly

CAPRA ✦ PRESS
MEMORABLE BOOKS SINCE 1969
SANTA BARBARA

A ROBERT BASON BOOK
Published by Capra Press
815 De La Vina Street
Santa Barbara, CA 93101
www.caprapress.com

Cover photograph © 2002 by Frank Goad
Cover design and book design by Frank Goad

Library of Congress Cataloging-in-Publication Data

Barre, Richard.
The Star / by Richard Barre.-- 1st ed.
p. cm.
ISBN 1-59266-008-8 (hardcover)
ISBN 1-59266-009-6 (hardcover numbered)
ISBN 1-59266-010-X (hardcover lettered)
1. African American boys--Fiction.
2. Motion picture actors and actresses--Fiction.
3. Los Angeles (Calif.)--Fiction.
I. Title.
PS3552.A73253 C48 2002
813'.54--dc21
2002012944

Edition: 10 9 8 7 6 5 4 3 2 1

First Edition

FOREWORD

Michael Connelly

I USED TO BE AGAINST THEM. I used to have a chip
on my shoulder. I was biased. I was even prejudiced.
I'm talking about short stories. I didn't write them, I
didn't read them. At least since I'd become a so-called
professional. My thinking was that if an idea or a char-
acter or even both weren't worth a good 300 pages of
exploration then they just weren't worth my time. Plain
and simple, but that's the way it was.

That was then and this is now. I am reformed
now. I'm in the church. A few years ago my so-called
professional responsibilities brought me to the collect-
ed works of Edgar Allan Poe. The big man himself. The
master. And of course, his work is shot through with
the short form. I had read these stories before. Many of
them. In my early years—before I took on the mantle
of the professional writer. I thought reading them again

would be a chore. But I was very wrong. Reading them again was like coming home to the things that made me want to become a professional. It was like being baptized in sacred waters. I saw the light.

Or rather, I saw the power. I understood again the secret of how less could be more. How in economy there is craft and no brevity of important and moving ideas. I knew that the short story had the power of all the emotions. The power to pierce, to tug, to scare. To make one think and feel something new.

Like all biases, mine was stupid and born of ignorance. I am over that now. I now try my hand in the same fields plowed so nobly by people like Poe. I am far behind but not deterred.

Richard Barre is *not* far behind. He has known the secret for a long time. He's plowed this field before and his rows are nice and straight. This story reminds me of Poe in many ways. A house with an aura, a cloak of the seemingly sinister underworld. A man of intrigue and mystery. A young person full of curiosity and hope. There is a spooky polish rubbed over all of this, onto every surface until it shines. Barre knows what he is doing and this story shows it. Edgar would be proud because it ripples with the muscle of less being more.

The Star

I WENT BACK THE OTHER DAY. No reason, really, other than it had been a while. Maybe it was the weather, one of those hazy days after Thanksgiving that make L.A. seem as if it's still smoldering from the fire season...like a pile of leaves being consumed without flames, the smoke rising up around the streetlights and making your eyes water.

The way it used to be when Marshalk lived in the house.

I sat looking at it in the twilight. It was always sort of a mongrel—Southwest plaster and tile slapped onto a late-teens California bungalow, the kind with the open-book roof jutting out to create a porch where occupants might watch the neighbors and relish an evening breeze, such as there was. But somewhere in the thirties this one had caught Santa Fe fever and the result was, well, unusual—the best or worst of both styles, I couldn't tell which. At any rate, with its double-lot width and protruding front window, it stood out among the singles and twenties-vintage clapboards around it.

Especially in 1953. When I was twelve and we lived next door.

Me, Naomi, and Mama.

I lit a cigarette with the car lighter and squinted out through the smoke. What used to be ours was gone now, knocked down and rebuilt to look like something that might house a large pair of shoes. But that wasn't why I was there…

My eyes went back to the Marshalk place.

I was glad I hadn't come during the day; with no lights on, the house's age receded as though mercifully veiled. Gaps showed in the curving tile roof. A realtor's sign stuck up near the front window, barred now, reflecting the times. Cracks laced the stucco facade, and on one wall some lunkhead had sprayed a homeboy slogan.

Richard Barre

Beside the drive, the giant deodar, once so full and droopy, looked stark against the twilight sky.

Which reminded me.

I looked up, searching for the star, but it wasn't dark enough to see yet. That was okay, I could wait. And remember.

✧

"Byron Whitaker, you get in this house right now."

"*Maa—it's still light.*" Mothers. I tried again: "Lukie and Clifford's mom lets them—"

"You want me to tan your hide in fronta the neighbors?" The ultimate threat, even though I could outrun her. Still, I had to eat sometime, and she knew it. Speed didn't count for beans then.

"Lydell and Chondra invited me to come watch TV," I said, knowing I was done but hoping for deliverance. Everybody I knew had a TV, surely everyone in Leimert Park.

Everyone but us.

"There's gonna be a Christmas special on—"

"*Gonna be one sorry boy on this block in*

about one minute."

"Coming," I said in my most devastated voice.

"Nighty night, Byron," the gaggle of kids intoned to my back. *"By—ron."*

I trudged up the stairs, banged the screen and slumped into a kitchen chair. Mama was feeding Naomi something from a jar that made her mouth orange. The baby's big dark eyes regarded me for a second then looked to the spoon for more. Her stumpy pigtails were tied off with little ribbons, making her face appear round. I sniffed, scanned the stove: tomato soup and cheese sandwiches again.

"Damn, Mama, see what you done now. Kids think I'm a baby."

"Who you hanging out with, talkin' like that?" she said without taking her eyes off Naomi. "And don't gimme that look, neither. We don't cuss in this house."

I wiped my face on my T-shirt sleeve, kick-ball sweat smudging dirt already there. Clearly there was no reasoning with this woman, not since Daddy left. For all I knew, I'd been switched at birth—I mean look at how much lighter my skin

was than hers, the way she hounded me constant-
ly. Made sense when you thought about it.

"I see you playing in the Marshalk yard?"

"No, Mama. Just looking for the ball." I'd
hoped it wasn't that obvious, what I was up to, but
there it was. A little flutter ran through me.

"Don't lie. One more time and your Daddy's
gonna hear about it. You'll *really* get it then."

"Oh, Mama, Daddy's gone for good and you
know it. Why else you workin' down at Johnson's?"

Johnson's Market needed black checkers to
make the neighborhood's increasing number of
Negro customers feel comfortable, and Mama applied
and was hired. Weeknights, she pulled evening
shifts after cafeteria work at Audubon School.
Which I swear was her way of keeping me in her
gunsights, seeing who I was eating with, if I'd finished my lunch, stuff like that. The eyes of a hawk,
that woman. Disposition too, lately.

"Why? So you can eat good and still be
ungrateful." She ladled the soup into a bowl, handed it to me on a plate with my cheese sandwich cut
into quarters.

I blew on the soup, spooned it around.

"You keep away from Marshalk's, the man ain't well. Mr. Titus said so. Are you listening, Byron? I'm serious."

"Yes, ma'am."

As she talked, she kept one eye on Naomi, who was fussing and grabbing for a bite of sandwich. At fifteen months, Naomi was my personal cross—my responsibility to pick up from the Cooley's where she spent the day, then take care of until Mama got home at eleven on weeknights.

"Mind your sister good tomorrow, I think she's coming down with something. You done your homework yet?"

"No, ma'am. Left it for tonight so it'll be fresh in my mind Monday. Good thinking, huh?"

She shook her head slowly. "Think about this, little man. Dishes, homework, bath, bed—in that order. Are we clear on that?"

I nodded, wondering how hard it would be to find my daddy once I set out to, once I got the money. No worse than living here, that was certain. Feeling like I couldn't breathe.

Not long now, I told myself. Later on, lying under the covers, my eyes open in the dark and hearing Mama's snores, I thought about how it was going to play out with Marvin Hall, Artie Bingham, and Raymo Combes. My co-conspirators.

The plan was to go over the back wall at ten. That way Naomi'd be asleep and I'd be out with the money before Mama got home. We all knew it was in there somewhere. Had to be, a house that big, Marvin said. Gold too, likely. Whole bags of it.

Setting out for school, I eyed the Marshalk place, no way of seeing in because the drapes were pulled, like always. The outside was white and unlived-in looking, with none of the Christmas decorations other houses had. Titus's car wasn't there yet, but it would be—Mondays he did light housekeeping and cooked. Mama knew this because she sold Titus his groceries, him smiling at her while she rang up the prices and put 'em in bags, her smiling back at him.

Made me want to throw up when I saw it.

Nobody ever saw Mr. Ludwig Marshalk, though. Artie thought he was dead or that Titus had him locked up in there to get his money. But

Titus wasn't there at night when the house was dark. That's all we had to know.

Raymo kept saying I'd be scared. But who'd be scared of somebody named *Ludwig*. Somebody I'd never even seen.

"Hey, punk." Marvin surprised me as I passed an alleyway near the school. He was tall, three years older than me, and long out of Audubon. Supposed to be going to Crenshaw High—when he felt like it, I guess. Didn't have a father either, something I could appreciate even though Marvin was kind of a bully and got in fights. But who better to have on your side?

Anyway, Marvin spent most of his time smoking the cigs he kept in his rolled-up sleeves, taking money off the younger kids, and hanging out with Artie and Raymo. Who emerged behind him.

"Look who's here," Artie said. "Lord Byron." Artie was a year behind Marvin at Crenshaw and Raymo was a grade ahead of me at Audubon, which was my connection. Lord Byron was a white wrestler who wore tights and stuff in the ring.

Artie nailed me one on the shoulder, but I didn't rub. I mean that was Artie, strong as a bear and built like one. Raymo was more my size, slight, with eyes that kept going back and forth between Marvin and Artie.

"*Lord By-ron,*" he echoed. He giggled, amused with himself—like a girl, I thought, but didn't say anything. See, Raymo had a switchblade.

"Shut up, Ray." Marvin glowered at me. "You tell anybody about tonight, punk?"

"Hey, I ain't no snitch."

"You scared, *By-ron?*" Artie said.

"Take more than that."

Marvin waved Artie off. "You straight on this, Byron? You're inside the basement window, you unlock the back door, we take it from there. You got that?" Marvin pinched my shoulder muscle where it met my neck.

"*Yes,*" I let out.

"Like takin' candy from a sleeping baby," he said, letting me go.

"What you gonna do with your share, By-ron?"

Before I could answer Raymo, Marvin said, "Gonna find his old man, aren't you Byron?" A strange light came into his eyes. "You guys believe that? What a waste. Tell him about *your* old man, moron. About him and your sister."

"Come on, Marvin," Raymo whined. "And don't call me moron, okay? I don't like it."

Marvin's punch was so quick I didn't even see it. But there was Raymo, doubled up on the ground and gasping.

"Sure, fool," Marvin said, winking at us. "Anything you say."

Artie laughed like crazy, but I noticed he stayed out of range.

So they might not have been pals exactly. But a man had to put aside childish things if he was ever going to grow up, right? If I was ever going to find Daddy and live with him, I needed the cash to do it. As Artie said once, money talks and bullshit walks. Everything would fall into place once I got the means.

School dragged by. At recess, I saw Raymo over by the fence, but I kept my distance and so did he. Afterward, I took the long way home so's not to get distracted by the other kids, then I was picking up Naomi at the Cooley's.

"She's fussy today. Got a drippy nose, too," Mrs. Cooley said. "You tell your mama, Byron."

"Yes, ma'am, I'll tell her."

Naomi squawked as I grabbed her away from the crayons, and she hollered all the way home. I fed her the Gerber's Mama'd left out for me to warm up, gave her a bath, and waited for her to fall asleep.

It was like somebody'd wound her up with a key—gimme this, gimme that, bouncing up and down in her crib when I tried to lay her down. Eight o'clock came, then nine and nine-thirty. I kept looking at Marshalk's, and sure enough the lights went off at nine, like always. But with Naomi still carrying on, Marshalk might not be asleep when we went in.

Then what?

I put on a dark shirt and pants, like Marvin said. I watched the second hand circle the electric clock. I went to the bathroom. I tried to see behind Marshalk's, where I was supposed to meet the guys, but saw nothing even though I knew they were there. Waiting.

Naomi howled in her crib. Finally at five minutes after ten, no less, she shut up and I was out the door and into the alley.

Marvin grabbed me roughly. "Oughta pound you, makin' us wait like that." Artie and Raymo mumbled assent. "You bring the flashlight?"

I showed him I had.

"Then let's go." He made a cup with his hands that I stepped into and hoisted me to the top of the wall. It was slick from dew, and for a minute I thought I was going to slip off, but I managed to steady up and drop feet first to the other side. We'd picked a night when there was no moon, and it took a second to get my bearings. I was in a garden, alongside a big barrel cactus I'd missed by inches. On my left, a path led to a patio and the house. The gate out to the alley was to my right.

I slid the bolt and let Marvin, Artie, and Raymo through.

"Damn it's dark," Raymo said.

"Shut up, fool. Byron, don't use the flash till you're inside. Signal us from the back door, okay?"

"Okay. But watch out for cactus. There's one right—"

"*Owww*," Artie said. "Son of a—"

"Go, Byron."

I went. The basement window was the key, spotted when the guys were over one day hatching the plan. I eased over there, looking indirectly at it the way I'd learned in scouts before I had to quit because of no money. The window looked small, but that's why I got the job. None of the others would have made it.

It was locked. Just as we expected.

I took out the little glass cutting tool Artie'd shown me how to use and etched a circle around where the latch was. But the little suction thing wasn't wet enough or something, and when I tapped the glass it fell out on the ground and broke.

I froze, expecting a hand to come out and grab me; thank God none did, because I'd have died right there. Finally I started to breathe again, and I saw the vague outline of Marvin waving me on from the wall. Thinking hard about the money, I reached in and found the latch.

After all that it gave easily, the window propped open no problem, and I was inside the basement, trying to see something—anything. Lord, it was dark in there. I flipped on the flash. Boxes were everywhere and there was a taller wardrobe carrier I'd seen the movers hauling in. On shelves were smaller boxes, books, and jars. Across from me, the stairs led to a door.

I crept across the concrete floor and up, wondering what I'd do if the door was locked. So far, so good—it wasn't. I opened it, looked around. The kitchen: sink, stove, and refrigerator to my left; breakfast alcove on the right; large plant, a palm or something, in the corner. Dead ahead was the back door, its window looking out on the patio and garden.

I made my way toward it so I could unlock and signal. Almost home.

"Don't move, please. I have a gun." The voice was taut and lightly accented. It also scared the living hell out of me.

The flash dropped from my hands and rolled away. I was dead—in a dark house with no idea of who or what I was facing. "Gun" rang in my ears. Whoever it was was going to shoot me.

The lights came on and he stepped out from behind the palm.

He wasn't much bigger than I was, five-six or -seven, if that. He wore a fabric jacket of some kind, its reddish color vivid contrast to the palest face I'd ever seen. He looked *bleached.* Thin and bleached. Dark eyebrows made it even more pronounced; black eyes bored into, through me, and out the other side. My own eyes were on the small revolver he held in his left hand.

"I assume that clunk we just heard from outside was your friends abandoning you," he said.

I eyed the open door to the cellar, but he reached over and shut it. I'd already seen the bolt and chain on the back door. I looked down at my pants. It was bad.

"Seems you've had an accident," he said calmly, dropping the pistol into his other pocket. "Do you do this kind of thing often?"

I said nothing; what was there *to* say?

"Answer me, please."

"No," I managed, feeling awful.

"And may I assume your mother doesn't know you're here? *Byron Whitaker from next door.*"

Oh, God, he knew my name. My life was over—Mama'd kill me if he didn't. "No," I said. "I mean yes."

"I see." He thought a moment, the pause

letting me see how peaked he really was. The skin of his face was pulled back from prominent cheekbones and teeth that looked too large. I thought about pushing him over and running, but where?

He reached a decision. "I'm prepared to offer you a bargain. I advise you to take it, as I won't offer again."

I looked at him as a drowning man must look at a lifeboat.

"Here it is," he said. "You help me every day after school for a week, and I won't mention this to your mother. Agree and you're free to go. Otherwise..."

"*Deal,*" I squeaked. I couldn't believe it, I was getting out alive.

He picked up my flash and turned on the porch light, illuminating the back yard, wall, and gate. "If I don't see you tomorrow, I will go to your mother with this." He held up the flash. "As for tonight, be thankful you broke into Ludwig Marshalk's house and not someone else's." He slipped the chain off the back door and worked the bolt. "Now get out of here."

I did.

I'd just finished changing, rinsing the rank

smell out of my wet pants, when Mama got home. She'd been right: There was a God.

Marvin was mad. I could tell by the way he had my arm bent back.

"Gotta be more to it than that," he said.

"Yeah," Raymo echoed, licking his lips. "Talk, By-ron."

I told them again about the bargain. Finally Marvin let me go, and I rubbed the feeling back into my shoulder.

"Damn, this might be better anyway," Artie said to Marvin, who was thinking hard about this new development. "More time for the punk to find the guy's money. Whole week."

Marvin and Raymo joined Artie in a smile as it dawned on them.

Looking at their faces, I felt like the beef in a roast beef sandwich.

At first we were wary of each other, Ludwig Marshalk and I, but it passed. He seemed to know that I had to mind the baby, and he let me bring her over after Titus was gone—back door, of course, so nobody'd know and mention it to Mama, arouse her suspicions. Even had a little area set up for Naomi and things for her to play with.

The house was way different than ours and not just bigger. It had a sunken living room, tile on the floor, paintings and expensive things on the walls, matching furniture. Money there, all right. The drapes were kept closed as usual, but that was okay, kind of cozy feeling. Helped keep the house warm, he said, and it was—near 80 in there. But I figured that was more for his illness, whatever it was, and after a while I didn't even notice. Actually, he looked better than last time, as if somebody'd put makeup on him, but that couldn't be right since he was a man

Anyway, what he wanted me to do seemed simple enough, just organize his stuff from the basement while he sat in a chair and told me which was what. Clothes, furnishings, things he seemed anxious to get rid of, most of it old, like you'd see in a museum. Some I'd liked to have given Mama, but that would have put her wise. A lot we set out for the trash. Other stuff we set aside with names of people or charities.

Putting it in order, he said. But never more than three hours at a time. You could just see the fatigue draining his enthusiasm. And I never saw him eat.

About the third day I guess it was, Marvin still hounding me about Ludwig Marshalk's money, we hit the boxes of photographs. Piles of them that he wanted put by category into the albums he'd set aside for some library.

I'd seen photographs, even taken some with a Brownie camera of Daddy's before it broke, but I'd never seen anything like these. It was like looking into another place and time: black-and-white scenes, people in old-looking clothes and hair. Seemed like I asked about every one; it slowed our progress, but I didn't care. Strangely enough, neither did he.

Many were pictures of him as a boy in Romania, where he'd been born. Others were of his wife, darkly pretty even though her clothes were out of date. He didn't say much about her, except that she'd died a long time ago in 1917 of a virus—

her and their little boy. The boy was in the pictures, too, different ages up to about mine. A lot of these Mr. Marshalk just shook his head at, as though I wasn't there.

Movie scenes he had a ton of; stills, he called them. Others had actors in poses, with autographs and little notes. Some pretty personal.

"How do you have these?" I asked. "Were you in the movies?"

"Not exactly," he said, running a hand over thinning hair. "I knew someone in silent films."

I'd seen a silent film one Saturday morning at the Leimert Theater, cops racing around or something. Silly without the sound.

"Who are all these addressed to? I-G-O-R..."

"Igor Lantz. You wouldn't know him."

"Why, is he dead?"

"Quite." He rummaged and came up with a scary-looking full-length portrait of a man all in black posed beside a crypt. Shadows obscured most of his face, but the eyes gave me chills. They burned out at the camera as if to say, "No place to hide, sucker. You're mine."

"Was this guy a real vampire or what?"

"No, it was just a part he was known for. *Nosferatu.*"

"Say what?"

He spelled it for me. "You like the movies?" *Moovez,* it sounded like when he said it, something I was getting used to, like the heat.

"Sure, when I have the money. Who doesn't?"

He reached into his pocket, came out with a five-dollar bill, which he put in my hand. "Go— take a friend. Enjoy yourself."

I was speechless. Here I'd busted into the guy's house, broke his window, was still looking to rob him, and he gives me—

"You earned it, Byron. A man needs to earn his place in the world. Now enough for one day, I'm tired."

So it went through the end of the week, the one right before Christmas vacation started. The one where I was going to take the money I hadn't found yet and go find my father.

We'd finished the photos and were almost through with the last box when I pulled out two things that looked like braces you strapped onto your legs. Like stilts, but shorter.

"Where you want these?" I asked.

He thought, looking tireder than I'd seen him all week. "Over there by the wardrobe. A costume shop might take them."

"You ready to do the wardrobe now?"

He looked at the six-foot-tall carrier tied up with rope. "No. We won't be doing that."

Seemed strange, leaving one undone. "How come?" I asked.

"Just a lot of old dead things. I'll tell Titus—" He sagged in the chair.

"Mr. Marshalk?" I stepped closer, but his eyes had shut and his mouth was open. His breathing sounded heavy, like Mama's when she drifted off on the couch.

My big chance to look for places where he might've hid his cash: closets upstairs that had looked promising, under his mattress, other spots I'd seen when he showed me the house. I raced up the stairs and was about to open the hall closet when something stopped me, I don't know what. Maybe it was the way he looked. Small and helpless.

I got a glass of water from the kitchen and went back down.

He wasn't in the chair. Prickles shot up and down my back.

"Is that for me?" He was leaning against the far wall by the broken window, sucking in fresh air. He held out a bony arm. I brought him the water, my eyes still wide.

"Sorry to frighten you," he said after downing some. "I thought you were upstairs going— gone, I mean."

"What happened to you, passin' out like that?"

"Just a little problem I have. Goes with getting old." He took his hand off the wall, stood, tottered, steadied.

"Are you okay?"

"Take tonight off, Byron, and we'll finish up Saturday. That should do it."

I helped him up the stairs and left, wondering what really happened down there.

Saturday afternoon, Marvin found the five

bucks.

"Big money for such a little guy, don't you think?" he said going through my jacket. His eyes got hard and mean. "Your Mama didn't give you no five bucks, that's for sure."

I watched his fist swing lazily up, and the next thing I knew I was in the dirt, my nose bleeding and Marvin right over me. "That's a sample of what we give guys who hold out on us," he said, the cigarette dangling from his mouth.

Raymo pressed the switch on his knife and the blade flicked out. He handed it to Marvin, who held it at my neck. "The only reason I don't cut your head off right now is because you know where things are in that house. Now I'm tired of waiting. Be in the alley tonight, 'cause we're going in. All of us."

He drew the blade lightly across my throat.

"Old man Marshalk better not give us no trouble either."

Mama left for work at four, checking my puffed nose before she left. Kickball in the face, I told her, had to happen sometime.

"Never seen you take one on the nose before, Byron. You been brawlin'?"

"No ma'am," I lied. Wasn't a lie, actually. Brawling takes two, and I wasn't stupid enough to take a swing at Marvin. "Have a good shift," I said as she went out the door.

For some reason I felt a lump in my throat when she left. Probably the bop I took. Naomi was still fussy from her cold, but unlike Monday she dropped off to sleep at seven, which was good because I wasn't about to take her to Marshalk's with me. One Whitaker in danger was enough, thank you.

"Whatever happened with those boys, Byron, the ones who took off on you?" We were just finishing up, marking some last items for Mr. Titus to dispose of, when he asked. Maybe he'd seen how distracted I was, what with Marvin, Artie, and Raymo likely outside the wall right now, and me wondering what the hell I was going to do about it.

"Oh, I don't know," I said. "They're around."

"It's always harder to do the right thing," he said after a bit. "Especially when the rest of the world is bigger than you are. Believe me, I know."

I didn't say anything, just felt small.

"There'll always be bullies. And not enough people to stand up to them. It's what they feed on, like vampires."

We went upstairs then, and suddenly the house felt very hot. I wiped my forehead while Ludwig Marshalk went to get something from his bedroom. I checked the little mantle clock: almost ten.

I was thinking of telling him the whole thing when he emerged from the hallway. In his hand was a squarish flat package, which he gave me.

"What is it?" I asked dumbly.

"You've never seen a Christmas present before?"

"But I don't have anything for you."

"The basement, that's my present. Now I can—prepare." His eyes looked especially bright and there was a flush on his neck.

"Prepare for what?"

"Nothing. Come over by the window. He surprised me by turning off the light. "Look up there. See that one just to the left of the Pleiades?"

"The what?"

"Those stars there. That one to the left."

Naturally, I thought this was odd. "So?" I said, spotting it, thinking his condition had caught up with his brain.

"Somebody gave it to me a long time ago. It's a lucky star. Now I'm giving it to you."

What do you say to that? I looked at it, then at him, back at it.

"Talk to it, give it a name. Or don't if you can't. But that would be a shame, because it works."

"Then why you giving it away?"

"Because it's time. And speaking of that, I think you had better go. Merry Christmas, Byron," he said quietly. "We're finished here."

When I closed the gate, it was as if I'd stepped into a horror film. Marshalk had killed his lights when I left, so the alley was all shadows. Branches hung down and strewn junk made eerie shapes. Even worse, mist had started to gather— damp as a wet sheet and smelling like one, dripping off the leaves. I tried to find the star, but couldn't through the trees.

Maybe they weren't waiting there, maybe they hadn't—

Marvin grabbed my arm, scaring the crap out of me.

"*There is no money, Marvin,*" I yelped. "*We were wrong.*"

"What'd I tell you," Artie said. "The little shit's cut us out."

"Guess so," Marvin said. "And after everything we told him, too."

The first blow knocked the breath out of me, the next whanged off my ear. I staggered, gasping, and the next one put me down. They were on me then, hitting me while I tried to roll myself into a ball. Finally Marvin, I guess it was, yanked me to my feet and drove a fist into my face. On my knees, I gagged, spat broken teeth and blood. A final kick bounced me off Marshalk's wall and into semi-consciousness.

From far off, I heard the click of the switch-blade and Raymo saying, "Yeah, do it, Marvin. Then the old man."

I managed to look Marvin in the face and blubber something about not hurting Mr. Marshalk, that he was sick, then I heard the gate swing open behind us and Marvin's eyes rose from me and got huge. "*Sweet Jesus,*" he said. "What is *that?*"

Artie made a strangled sound beside him and fell back. Somebody moaned, Raymo I think.

Still dazed, I managed to look behind me. The thing was at least seven feet tall, all in black and caped. Its head was bald and skull-like, its ears pointed, the eyes huge and terrifying. Slowly it revealed fangs that were red with blood. Then it raised one talon-like finger at Marvin.

"Oh God, please, no," he croaked.

That's when I passed out.

I have no idea how, but I was on the couch when Mama came home from work, took one look at my face and screamed bloody murder. Finally I got her calmed down. But I had to tell her about

Marvin, Artie, and Raymo beating on me for some money I earned from Mr. Marshalk. Trying to get enough to buy her a Christmas present is how I put it, my fingers crossed behind my back.

She burst into tears then and held me, but I was glad when I finally got to bed, the aspirin she'd given me making me feel a little better.

Next day she went after my attackers.

Artie's and Raymo's parents were alternately apologetic to her and mad at them, she said, and they must have come down hard because I had no further trouble with either of them. Raymo avoided me altogether at school. Artie stuck close to Crenshaw.

As for Marvin, we heard he went to live with a cousin out of state. Which apparently was more or less okay with Marvin's mother and the eight other kids in the Hall family. Guess Marvin wasn't too popular there, either.

Ludwig Marshalk and I never spoke again. Two days before Christmas, we had a visit from Mr. Titus, who told us our neighbor had died of advanced pernicious anemia, a rare blood disorder that made him so weak his heart stopped.

Richard Barre

"The poor man," Mama said.

"Yeah, he really went downhill after the weekend," Titus said. "Couldn't even lift his head."

Mama went in the kitchen to get Titus some tea and homemade cookies. After she'd gone, Titus handed me a package from under his coat. Dirt was on the wrapping and one corner had a rip, but I recognized it right away. He said, "This was on Mr. Marshalk's desk with a note to give it to you personally and confidentially. Said you'd dropped it." He looked at me as though expecting I'd tell him all about it, man to man or something.

"Thanks, Mr. Titus," I said. Then I went to my room.

Of course it was the picture of *Nosferatu*. But what made me sad, opening it in my room on Christmas morning in 1953 before Mama and Naomi were even out of bed, the house all quiet, was the writing he'd put on it: *To Byron, who proved to be very tall indeed. From your friend, Ludwig Marshalk (Igor Lantz).*

I hoped my tears wouldn't lower me in his

eyes if he happened to be watching.

Jingle Bells coming from somewhere snapped me out of it. I took a last drag on the cigarette, crushed it in the ashtray, craned my head out the car window. It was quite dark now and cool, and mist was starting to rise off the damp lawns and gather in the low spots.

And there it was—the lucky star he'd given me so long ago.

Did it work as he said? Not with my dad when we finally did get together. But then maybe his new wife and situation had more to do with that, her having three kids and all. At any rate, it helped Mama over some rough spots, and even though I couldn't see it in Vietnam, I felt it up there, keeping me in one piece when I was so scared I couldn't get my breath. My fellow sufferers in the acting profession might consider two academy award nominations a pretty fair track record, too. See, Marshalk gave me that as well. I mean if I didn't know what an academy award performance was after seeing him in action, who did?

I cast a final look upward, smiled at Ludwig and turned the key. Driving away, I made a mental note to call the realtor whose phone number was on that sign.

Just for luck, you understand.

One thousand hardcover copies of *The Star* were printed by Capra Press in October 2002. One hundred and fifty copies have been numbered and signed by the author and Mr. Connelly. Twenty-six copies in slipcases were also lettered and signed by both.

About Capra Press

Capra Press was founded in 1969 by the late Noel Young. Among its authors have been Henry Miller, Ross Macdonald, Margaret Millar, Edward Abbey, Anais Nin, Raymond Carver, Ray Bradbury, and Lawrence Durrell. It is in this tradition that we present the new Capra: literary and mystery fiction, lifestyle and city books. Contact us, we'd love to hear from you.

815 De La Vina Street, Santa Barbara, CA 93101
805 892-2722 • www.caprapress.com